Stop!

Before you turn the page —
Take a piece of paper.
Pick up your pencil.
Draw a big triangle.

At the top point of the triangle write **Secret Government UFO Test Base**. At the left point write **Dinosaur Graveyard**. At the right point, **Humongous Horror Movie Studios**. And in the exact center of the triangle write, **Grover's Mill**.

Ah, Grover's Mill. A perfectly normal town, bustling with shops, gas stations, motels, restaurants, and schools. A small town with a great big heart, nestled snugly in the midst of —

Wait! Did we say *normal*? A studio where they film the cheapest horror movies ever made? The world's largest and smelliest graveyard of ancient dinosaur bones? A secret army base filled with captured alien spacecraft?

All this makes poor Grover's Mill the exact center of supreme intergalactic weirdness!

Turn the page.
If you dare.
Enter The Weird Zone!

There are more books about

THE WEIRD ZONE

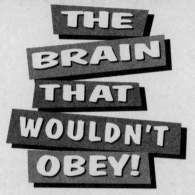

THE WEIRD ZONE

THE BRAIN THAT WOULDN'T OBEY!

by Tony Abbott

Cover illustration by Broeck Steadman
Illustrated by Lori Savastano

A
LITTLE APPLE
PAPERBACK

SCHOLASTIC INC.
New York Toronto London Auckland Sydney

For Linnea and Jane

ISBN 0-590-67437-4

Text copyright © 1997 by Robert Abbott. Illustrations copyright © 1997 by Scholastic Inc. All rights reserved. Published by Scholastic Inc. LITTLE APPLE PAPERBACKS and the LITTLE APPLE logo are registered trademarks of Scholastic Inc.

12 11 10 9 8 7 6 5 4 3 2 1   7 8 9/9 0 1 2/0

Printed in the U.S.A.   40

First Scholastic printing, January 1997

Contents

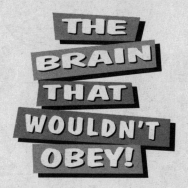

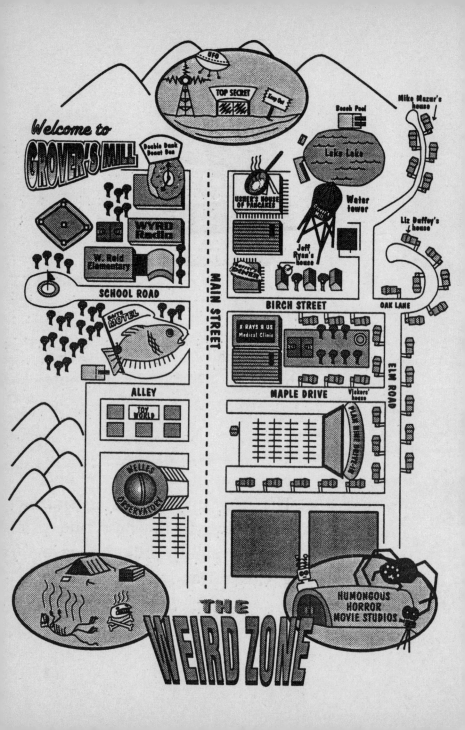

If I Only Had a . . .

By the time Mike Mazur saw the greasy french fry bag, it was already too late.

Wump! Bump! Dump! Splat!

"Owww!" Mike cried out as he tumbled down the school bus steps. He rolled onto the sidewalk in front of W. Reid Elementary School.

Mike peeled the Jolly Meal french fry bag from the bottom of his sneaker and looked up. The bus driver was tossing another empty fry bag to the floor under his seat. With his mouth full, he gave Mike a shrug, closed the door, and roared off.

"Thanks for the ride . . . I think!" Mike

groaned. He limped up the school steps and through the main doors.

At once, he felt a tingle of excitement. A giant banner rippled above the entrance to the gym.

W. Reid Science Fair Today!
Win First Prize!

"I can see it all now!" Mike mumbled as he burst into the gym. "I win first prize, do lots of TV interviews, and become the most famous scientist in the world. Cool!"

Mike grinned and whispered into the lunch bag he was carrying, "And it'll all be because of you."

Dozens of tables were set up on the gym floor. There were already lots of science projects lined up. Mike smiled as he walked past the other kids' projects. *Three-Sided Triangles. The Amazing Bottle of Air. Dirt + Water = Mud.* None of the other projects seemed quite as brilliant as his.

"Zoners," he thought to himself. *Zoners* was the word his friends used to describe nearly everyone in Grover's Mill. Mike was pretty new to town, but he had to agree that Grover's Mill was definitely the Zone.

The Weird Zone.

The absolute center of intergalactic weirdness. A place where, if two things could happen, a weird thing and a regular thing, the weird thing would always happen.

Mike set the bag on his table and whispered to himself, "And the first prize goes to . . ."

". . . Liz Duffey!" said a voice behind him.

Mike turned on his heel just in time to see his friend Liz Duffey glide past him. Her long blonde hair floated in the air behind her.

Mike glanced at her feet. Liz was riding on a skateboard. A tiny motor on the back was powering the wheels. Liz rode down one aisle and back up the next. She stopped in front of Mike's table and hopped to the floor.

"I'm going places on *my* project," she said with a smile. "I call it — Motorboard!"

"Nice work, Liz," Mike said. "I'm glad you're here. Because today will go down in history."

Mike opened his bag and stuck his hand in.

"The history of weirdness," said Liz. "I mean, did you look at these science projects? *How Water Drips! See-Through Glass?*" She shook her head. "Pretty zoney, Mike."

"At least you and I have good stuff," Mike said. He grinned as he pulled out a red plastic box and set it on the table.

"Wait," said Liz. "Is that a radio? Mike, I hate to tell you. Radio has already been invented."

Mike snickered with delight. "Not just a radio." He pulled out a dusty brown baseball-sized potato from the bottom of his bag. "A potato-powered radio. I call it — *Potadio!*"

Liz watched as Mike slowly pushed wires from the radio right into the potato. "The acid from the potato is changed into

electricity," he said. "It's like nature's battery. Cool, huh?"

"Not bad," said Liz, pulling a tissue from her pocket and blowing her nose. "Can you get hockey scores?"

Mike shrugged. "So far it just picks up WYRD, the Grover's Mill station. It's kind of faint."

"Well, I probably won't hear it," mumbled Liz. "My cold has stuffed my ears."

The gym was starting to fill up. Mike saw Mrs. Carbonese taking surprise snapshots for the yearbook. She wore a pink sweater and glasses on a string. Around her neck was a silver police whistle. She used it to get silence in her class.

Principal Bell was walking from table to table with his hands on his hips. Miss Lieberman, the assistant principal, was right behind him. She was making notes about everything he said.

"There's Jeff," Mike said to Liz, pointing to their friend Jeff Ryan as he set up his project.

"Let's see what he's got," said Liz. "By the way, I talked to Holly last night. She and Sean built some kind of *secret* project. I can't wait to see it."

The two kids stepped over to Jeff's table just as Principal Bell strolled by.

"Ahem!" boomed the principal, reading the sign on Jeff's table. "*The Gizmo*. Very good. Now, show us the magic of science! The wonder of invention! The terrific W. Reid spirit!"

"Yes, sir!" Jeff smiled big and slipped a pair of goggles over his face. He tapped a button on the base of the Gizmo and cried out, "Stand back!"

It was a good thing.

Zzzzz! Krrrr! Nnnn-chunka-chunka!

A sudden flash of prongs and nozzles and flippers screamed into action!

Nnnnnnn! The ceiling lights hissed and sparked and flashed as the Gizmo jumped and jumbled across the table, growling and grinding.

All the lights in the school dimmed and

flickered. The machine was a blur of horrible noise!

"What does it do?" Liz yelled over the sound.

Jeff gave her a blank look. "Do?"

Mike nodded. "Do. What does it do? To advance science?"

Jeff shut off his machine and the lights came back up. He gave another blank look. "Do?"

"Ahem!" said Mr. Bell, clearing his throat. "Very interesting. Next!" He and Miss Lieberman stepped over to another table.

"I guess I don't win anything," Jeff sighed, pulling his goggles off and staring at the Gizmo.

Mike patted him on the shoulder. "Only one person can win, Jeff. And I've got — *Potadio.*"

"Actually, son," Mr. Bell said, walking back over. "Your little radio doesn't seem to work at all."

Mike raced over to the table. He flipped the on switch over and over. Nothing. Not a sound.

Principal Bell put his hands on his hips and frowned at the radio. "I can see you and your vegetable need a moment. We'll be back."

Liz leaned over to Mike. "Why don't you just give that potato a good scrub? It's filthy."

"Great idea," said Mike. "Can't have dirt on the invention of the century!" He unplugged Potadio and dashed down the hall and into the bathroom. He ran the potato under warm water.

Lots of dirt washed off.

Mike wondered whether the potato felt the warm water like he did. Did potatoes have feelings like people? It was alive, after all. Potatoes do grow.

What are you washing me for?

Mike chuckled to himself. Wouldn't it be weird if the potato actually said that?

"Hey, kid, I asked you a question. You planning to cook me, or what? Don't eat me, pal."

Mike looked all around the room. It was empty. "Wait, who said that?"

But at that moment — *Ahhhhh!* — a horrible, bloodcurdling scream pierced the bathroom!

It was coming from the science fair!

It was coming from Liz!

Mike raced back to the science fair, clutching his damp potato. When he burst into the gym, he saw a huge metal machine smashing through the tables after Liz!

On the front of the machine was a big hand attached to a long metal arm. A powerful spring was coiled under the arm.

"Help!" Liz cried, as she fell against the bleachers. She kicked at the giant hand coming down at her. It moved closer and closer.

Mike dived. With one quick move he pushed Liz out of the way just as the metal hand lunged.

Errrrk! The machine stopped.

Flonk! A small slit opened on the top of the machine and two faces appeared.

Mike looked up at the faces. "Sean? Holly?"

The faces smiled. "Cool project, huh?" shouted Holly Vickers. "It's a catapult!"

"Thanks a lot, friends!" Liz snarled. She got up and dusted herself off.

Mr. Bell strode through the tables as Holly and her brother Sean popped out the top of the catapult and jumped down to the floor. "Ah, the glories of invention!" the principal boomed.

"And all from spare parts," said Holly.

"It can hurl objects hundreds of feet in the air," added Sean. He looked at Mike, who was still on the floor. "Let's try it with the potato that Mike's got." Sean reached for Potadio.

"No!" Mike cried. "That's my project!"

Sean raised his eyebrows. "Oh, sorry, Mike." Then he grinned. "Enormous metal catapult versus dusty little potato. Hmm. I wonder who'll win."

Mike glanced down at the small lump resting in his hand. Now that it was all clean, he noticed lots of scratches and scars all over it.

The potato looked kind of sad.

"Sorry, little spud," Mike whispered. "I guess you don't stand a chance against that big thing."

"Dad thinks our project is so good," said Sean, "he's going to make a movie with it. He's going to call it *Scary Evil Robot Ghost Gremlins from Another Scary Dimension!*"

"Because plain old regular gremlins just aren't scary enough," said Holly, with a smile.

Sean and Holly's father was Todd Vickers, the not-so-famous movie director and owner of Humongous Horror Movie Studios. His movies were scary, but usually not very good.

Suddenly, the doors of the gym flew open and in stepped a tall man. He had fluffy blond hair, a slim suit, and shiny black shoes.

The crowd of kids and teachers grew hushed.

"Who's that?" whispered one kid.

"Yeah, who?" whispered another.

The blond man stepped slowly to the center of the gym, holding up a microphone.

He squinted out across the crowd. He began to curl his lips into a wide grin. He raised an eyebrow slowly. Very slowly.

"Storm," he announced. "Rock Storm. That's my name and hosting is my game! I've come all the way from WYRD Radio to host your science awards show!" Then he looked around. "Hey, everybody — how's my hair?"

"Ahem!" Principal Bell said, walking over from the other side of the gym and bending over the microphone. "We're pleased to invite you to our display of junior scientific genius and — "

"Sure, sure, school-head-guy," Rock Storm broke in. "But let me do the announcing, okay?"

Rock Storm began by stepping over to Mike's table. Sean, Holly, and Jeff came over and stood next to Mike and Liz.

"Hey, look at this," said Rock, smirking down at the potato. "Is it lunchtime already? Ha-ha!"

"Actually, sir," Mike began, "these green sprouts here are called the eyes. And these wires convert the acid in the potato to electricity. I cleaned everything, so it should work now."

Mike inserted the final wire and flipped the switch on the transistor radio. The tiny round speaker sputtered. Little blue lines of electricity seemed to flash from the wires. The brown lump with green sprouty eyes wobbled on the table.

"It's gonna do it," Mike cried out. "Everyone, prepare to hear radio!" The speaker hummed. It squealed.

Eeeee! Everyone smacked their hands over their ears and winced at the high-pitched squeaking!

Mike twisted the radio dials. "It's coming!"

Just then, Mrs. Carbonese shuffled over. She held a little camera in front of her face. "Everybody — smile!"

FLASH!

The burst of light from the flash seemed to shoot right at the potato, and for an instant the wires glowed white, then red, then blue!

Mike blinked at the bright flash.

"My eyes! My eyes! Hey, watch that camera, lady! You trying to blind me?"

Everyone went quiet.

Mrs. Carbonese's face dropped.

Her camera dropped.

She pointed a sharp quivering finger at Mike, nearly sticking it up his nose. "This boy said rude words to me!" Then she fumbled for her police whistle and blew hard.

Woooooooo!

Everyone turned to Mike and frowned.

Mike turned to his potato and frowned.

3

The Power to Control the Mind!

"It wasn't me," cried Mike, pointing to his table. "It was him. The potato, the radio, Potadio!"

"Don't yodel at me, rude boy," cried Mrs. Carbonese. Then she picked up her camera and clacked off down the aisle in her high-heeled shoes.

Mr. Bell frowned deeply at Mike and moved on to another table with Rock Storm.

Mike turned to his friends. "Really, guys, it was him. The potato said that."

Liz shook her head and sighed. "Sure, Mike."

"He talked to me before, too," Mike went

on. "When I was washing him in the bathroom."

"Right," said Sean with a laugh. "And what did he say? 'Don't eat me.'?"

Mike blinked at Sean. "Actually, he did."

Jeff nodded. "Well, if I were a vegetable and somebody was washing me, that's probably what I would say. 'Don't eat me.' You know?"

Liz made a face. "This is too weird for me. We're talking about a potato, okay? They don't talk. They can't think. They're just lumpy food."

"Of course I'm in a grumpy mood," Mrs. Carbonese snapped back over her shoulder. "That rude boy said bad words to me." She stared at Mike as if she were going to blow her whistle again, then she clacked off between the tables.

Liz looked at her friends and tapped her ears. "Mrs. C. is sort of hard-of-hearing."

"Now, let's get going, people!" Rock Storm boomed into the microphone. "I've got a call-in show in half an hour. Wouldn't want the world to miss that!"

Principal Bell, Miss Lieberman, and Mrs. Carbonese went up on the stage with the announcer.

"It's time for the big prize to be awarded," Rock Storm said. "And I think we all agree that one project here today is quite an achievement."

Mike glanced at the big catapult towering over all the other projects. He saw Sean smile at his sister, breathe on his fingernails, and buff them on his shirt. They're going to win, thought Mike.

His little Potadio didn't look so great anymore. He ran a finger across a gash in the potato's skin. "I wonder if it hurt when he got that."

Liz turned. "Don't get weird on me, Mike. It's a vegetable, not a pal. But, listen, with my ears all stuffed up, I can't hear the awards. Let's get closer." She walked over to the stage.

Mike just kept looking down at the Potadio. "We'll never win."

Suddenly, tiny sparks began to shoot off the wires connecting the vegetable to the radio.

Zzzz! Sput! Sput! The sparks flashed white, blue, and red and rippled along the wires.

The potato began to twitch on the table.

"Hey!" Mike leaned over. "What's going on?"

The radio's speaker began to crackle and hiss. Then it made a sound. "Pssssst!"

"Huh?" Mike put his ear to the speaker.

"Pssst!" the thing hissed again. Then the potato twitched a little. Then it spoke. "Hey, Mike!"

Mike's eyes went wide. His mouth fell open.

"Yeah, kid, I'm talking to you!" the potato hissed. "Your name's Mike, right?"

"Yeah . . . but . . . you're . . . you're . . . a . . ."

"Well, I'm not a grapefruit!" chuckled the

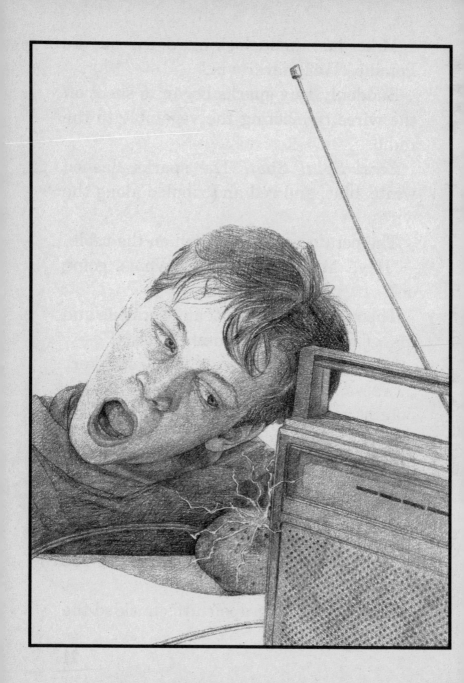

potato. "Listen, thanks for zapping me with all these wires and stuff. And that camera flash gave me a jolt of juice, too. Boy, I feel like a million bucks!"

"Uh-huh," said Mike, wondering if he was really hearing what he thought he was hearing.

"Hold on to your hat, Mikey boy," the potato said. "And watch this!"

Mike saw the vegetable's rough, brown skin wrinkle all over then stretch out, as if the potato were taking a deep breath!

All of a sudden — *Krrippp!* — the gash on the top of the potato split open! Underneath the rough skin was a ripply pink blob. It pushed itself up and began to throb. It bulged. It stretched.

"Is that a . . . ?" gasped Mike. "What is it?"

"Well, it's not my flavorful cheesy topping!" snorted the Potadio. "Now watch what happens when I do this!" The pink bulge began to turn purple as the potato groaned and twitched.

Suddenly, Rock Storm screamed out. "The winner is — is — is — ungh! — *the Potadio!*"

"Whoa!" shrieked Mike, jumping up and down. "I can't believe it! This is so cool!"

At that moment, Principal Bell, Miss Lieberman, Rock Storm, and all the other teachers rushed down from the stage and crowded around Mike and his Potadio.

They slapped their ears and began to sing.

Oh, wondrous Potadio,
Not just a radio,
  But so much more!

"What? What?" Liz stammered, squeezing through the crowd. "Everyone's gone Zoner!"

And the Zoners sang a second verse!

Oh, don't you nibble
This veg-a-tibble!
  He's so much more!

The potato's pink bulge went purple again.

Suddenly, Rock Storm's head jerked back. He raised the microphone to his lips. "Yes, master!" he murmured. "At once, master!"

The announcer grabbed Liz's skateboard, jumped on, started the motor, and roared off through the tables.

"Hey!" cried Liz. "He's stealing my project!"

Going Shopping?

Without another word Principal Bell snatched Potadio off Mike's table, raised him high in the air, and brought him up to the stage.

He's so much more! everyone sang.

"This is getting weird," said Mike.

"Weird is the word," cried Liz. "I'm going after Rock Storm. And you're coming with me!"

Mike paused. "But my Potadio . . ."

Liz dragged him to the door. "Your dumb potato will be fine, Mike. Let's go!"

"You probably shouldn't call him dumb," mumbled Mike, running after Liz. "He talks."

When they got outside, Rock Storm was racing down School Road toward Main Street. "Yes, master," he droned. "I will, master!"

He rode Liz's skateboard as if he were in a daze, zigzagging on and off the sidewalk.

Liz looked back over the top of the school at the WYRD radio tower. She pulled a tissue from her jeans pocket and wiped her nose. "It doesn't look like he's going back to WYRD."

The tall blond radio announcer with the big voice shot across Main Street. He jumped up onto the sidewalk on the other side. Then he jerked around and stared behind him.

Liz blew her nose hard.

"Duck!" said Mike.

Liz frowned. "That's not nice. I have a cold."

"No, I mean get down!" Mike pulled Liz behind a newspaper stand and peeked over.

Rock Storm scanned the street and

slipped into Pay & G'way, Grover's Mill's grocery store.

"He's going shopping," Mike said.

A few moments later, Rock Storm was out of the store and rolling back across the street. He carried a brown grocery bag. "Now, master, now!" he kept murmuring.

"Who's he talking to?" said Liz.

The announcer stumbled up the WYRD steps and disappeared behind the big glass doors.

"What do you think?" said Mike. "Maybe he's just out of Wheat-O cereal and needs more."

A moment later — *Krrzzzzz!* The reception dish on top of the WYRD building began to turn. Jagged sparks, almost like lightning, shot off it.

"Something's going on in there," said Liz. She trotted up the steps, pulled open the doors, and darted inside the building. "And I want my Motorboard back. Even if it didn't win a prize."

Inside, a hissing, buzzing sound filled the air.

"It's coming from down there," Mike whispered. He pointed to a room at the end of a hall. A strange, blue glow came from the doorway. Sparks sputtered and flew out the door.

"This is creepy," whispered Liz. "It's not normal. It's . . . weird science."

Mike knew exactly what she meant. He felt a twinge of something when he saw those sparks. They reminded him of his own science project.

They crept up to the room and peeked inside.

Rock Storm was babbling to himself as he fiddled over the big control board in front of him. He was bathed in a strange blue light.

Krrrzz! Sparks flew up all around him.

"Master," the man droned. "Your plan is working!" Rock Storm didn't even notice that there were two kids in the room with him.

Mike edged behind the announcer and peered around him. What he saw shocked him.

Potatoes! A dozen dusty brown spuds, sparking and sputtering and giving off a blue glow.

Wires ran from the potatoes straight into the control board and up to the radio tower broadcasting signals on top of the building.

Liz nudged Mike. "What's going on here?"

Mike frowned. "The potatoes. I think they're . . . they're . . . doing radio stuff?"

Bong! the clock on the Double Dunk Donut Den next door chimed the hour.

Sssss! the big pan on Usher's House of Pancakes across the street hissed the hour.

Rock Storm, his face blue in the glow of the sparking potatoes, flipped a switch on the control board. Then he slumped down in his chair.

"Welcome to the WYRD call-in hour," he droned. "Hello, caller. You're on the air."

A voice crackled from the speaker across the room. "Well, snap my suspenders and holler at my hogs!" said the voice. "My name's Farmer Tom. People call me Farmer Tom 'cause I'm a farmer, don't ya know!"

"And the reason for your call?" Storm droned.

"Well, I'm out in my field a minute ago, and — boom! The dirt flies up all around me and them critters just sorta rolled outta the ground and took off across my field! Hundreds of 'em."

Rock Storm just stared. Then his neck began to twitch, and his eyes started rolling around.

"Um . . . what critters, sir?" Mike said into the radio microphone.

"Why taters! Spuds! Po-ta-toes!" answered the voice of Farmer Tom. "Thousands of 'em."

Liz shot a look at Mike. She leaned into the microphone. "And can you tell us where the potatoes went?"

"That-a-way!" the farmer's voice answered.

"This is radio, sir," said Mike. "We can't see where you are pointing."

"Well, bust my laces and string my fiddle!" Farmer Tom yodeled. "Over yonder! There! Straight to Grover's Mill!"

School Daze

Clank! The microphone slid from Mike's hand and hit the control board. A shiver of fear ran down his neck. "Potatoes? Coming here?"

Suddenly, a pair of hands grabbed Mike by the shoulders. "Master says, humans are bad!"

"Whoa!" yelled Mike. He tried to twist out of Rock Storm's grasp, but the announcer held tight. He swung Mike around and lifted him off the ground. Storm rolled his eyes, stuck his tongue in and out, and began blinking really fast. Really really fast.

"He's looking weird at me!" cried Mike,

his feet dangling below him. "I don't like it!"

In a flash, Liz yanked a potato from the control board and pitched it hard at the announcer.

"No!" screamed Rock Storm. He dropped Mike and caught the potato. He began to pet it.

"We're outta here!" cried Liz. She grabbed Mike, found her skateboard, and shot out the door. A second later they were on Main Street.

"What was that all about?" gasped Mike. Then he came to a dead stop. He looked down the street between WYRD and the Double Dunk Donut Den. Mike could see beyond the town to the desert spreading out to the west.

He had seen this same scene every morning from his school bus.

But something was different about it this time.

"Liz, look!" Mike pointed out to the flat brown distance. Dozens of little spirals of dust were coming from the west. "They're coming! Farmer Tom was right, potatoes are coming this way!"

The dust spirals grew into a dark cloud.

KRRZZZ! Wild sparks sputtered and shot off the radio tower and into the air.

"That's it!" cried Mike. "Radio waves. Just like my Potadio. It all makes sense."

"Not to me," said Liz, beginning to run.

"Rock Storm hooked the potatoes up to the broadcast tower," Mike began, keeping up with her. "Just like I hooked my potato up to the radio. My potato came alive. And so did these potatoes! They sent a signal to every other potato in the world. And they're all coming here!"

"Oh, right. That makes perfect sense," Liz said, as she tore around the corner of School Road. "Potatoes talking and sending signals? Sure. I mean this is the Zone, after all. And did your potato tell you why this is happening?"

"No, but I have a feeling we'll find out," Mike said. "Once we get back to school."

And something told Mike that what they would find at school would definitely not be good. The minute the two kids slammed through the school doors, Mike knew he was right.

The place was very quiet. The gym was empty. Jeff Ryan was standing alone in the front hall. He was wiggling his fingers in his ears and tapping his foot very fast. "Oooh!" he said. "Ahhh!"

"I have a bad feeling about this," said Mike.

Then Jeff held his hand up as if he'd just heard something. "Uh-huh. Okay. Yeah, sure. I'm coming!" He stumbled quickly down the hall, tapping his feet. "Oooh!" he droned. "Ahhh!"

"It's like he's hearing something," said Liz.

Before they could follow him, Sean and Holly came stumbling out of the cafeteria. Their hands were dripping with red stuff.

"Uh-oh. Now what?" mumbled Mike.

"Ketchup," Sean said, flicking his eyelids and scratching his ears. "We just emptied all the ketchup containers."

"That's . . . helpful," said Mike. "I guess."

"Uh, Holly . . ." Liz began.

"Don't call me Holly," said Holly, her voice starting to drone a little. "I'm Spudlet thirty-nine."

"I'm Spudlet forty-seven," droned Sean.

"All right, you guys," said Liz. "This is dumb. Joke's over. Ha-ha. Now, what's going on here?"

But Holly just turned to her brother, made a little fist with each hand, and shouted, "Spud!"

"Spud!" her brother shouted back.

Then they both stumbled down the hall after Jeff, muttering, "Yes, master!"

"I think I'm going to be majorly ill," said Liz. She looked down the hall where her three friends were heading. "Our friends are way weird and this is way not funny."

"Ha-ha-ha-ha!" Laughter came tumbling up the hall.

"Something's funny," said Mike. "Let's find out what."

The laughter was coming from Mrs. Carbonese's classroom. Liz and Mike ran up to the door. Kids were standing in a large circle around the teacher's desk.

A voice was coming from the circle. ". . . So I said, 'Who, me? I don't have any bananas!' "

The kids doubled over with hilarious laughter. When they did, Mike glimpsed a big brown lumpy thing sitting on the teacher's desk.

"Potadio!" shrieked Mike. "He got . . . big!"

It was Potadio, and he did get big. He was the size of a large watermelon now, and he had started to grow features.

A little mouth grinned and showed rows and rows of shiny white teeth. And here and there on the potato's skin were lots of green eyes, some of them growing out into long leafy sprouts.

But the grossest part was the lump on

top. The big pink bulge was much bigger and pinker and bulgier than before.

"Gross," groaned Liz. "With a capital G."

"Hey!" cried the potato, looking up. "Here's the boy who gave me my wake-up call! Welcome to my world, Mikey boy!"

"Uh, sure," Mike mumbled. He pointed to the bulge. "Is that really what I think it is?"

"If you're thinking megahuge brain, you'd be megahuge right!" Potadio said.

"You're controlling everybody, aren't you?" Liz asked, stepping back. "Aren't you?"

The potato snorted and jiggled. "With supersonic brain waves, I control people's thoughts, yes. With a dome like mine, it's a cinch. But right now, I've got bigger things on my mind."

Then one of Potadio's sprouts curled up like a hand and tapped the bulge on the top of his head. "Get it? *Bigger things on my mind*? Oh, I mash myself!"

The kids cracked up again.

"But seriously," said the potato, "how do you like the names Spudlet eighty-six and ninety-nine? Catchy, huh?"

"No way!" said Liz. "You're not getting us!" She grabbed Mike by the arm and pulled him back.

"Look into my eyes!" shrieked the potato.

Mike looked at the vegetable. "Which eyes?"

"Any of them, they all do the same thing!"

Mike looked. Then the potato with the brain squinted his many potato eyes and gritted his many potato teeth and held his potato breath.

His brain turned purple again.

A moment later, all the students in the classroom went nuts. Jeff rattled off the ABC's completely backward in a high-pitched voice.

Holly did back flips over the desks.

Sean began to do a dance from the sixties!

Mike shook his head. "This is very sad."

Potadio's eyes narrowed at Mike and Liz. "What's with you two? Don't you hear it?"

Liz shrugged. "Like what, for instance?"

"Like *eeeee*, for instance! Like my supersonic brain waves controlling your mind!" The vegetable's brain bulged bigger.

Mike listened. "Sorry, nothing. But then, I have an earwax problem."

Liz pulled away. "Well, that sounds yucky."

"So!" Potadio growled angrily. "If you won't be my spudlets, this means war!"

Potatoes Can Rock and Roll!

Suddenly — *clack-clack-clack!*

Mrs. Carbonese came running in the classroom door. She looked at the potato with the brain sitting on her desk. "Oh! Are you a substitute? Well, you are not needed today. I am here, thank you."

"Not for long!" cried Potadio. His brain bulged big again and one of his leafy arms jabbed out at the students. "Get her, spudlets!"

Jeff stopped his ZYX's and picked up a little green box from the teacher's desk. He opened it, and tossed bits of chalk to the other students.

Sean and Holly turned toward Mike and Liz. Their chalk bits were drawn like swords!

The others marched slowly toward Mrs. Carbonese.

"Wait," the teacher said. "I haven't given you the math problems yet!"

But the students kept coming. Jeff and the others stomped up the aisle, their fingers clutching sticks of chalk no longer than an inch!

Mrs. Carbonese stepped back. "Stop or I will blow my whistle," she warned.

But the students kept coming.

Mrs. Carbonese backed into the blackboard. The sweater fell off her shoulders! Her glasses tumbled to the desk! Her whistle slipped from her lips!

"Take your seats this instant!" she shrieked.

But they didn't. And in that instant, Mike realized that this was a battle of good against evil.

And evil was winning.

"We can't let this happen!" Mike cried out. "Liz, block for me!"

Liz barreled forward against Sean and the other students. Mike dived between desks to the front of the room and grabbed Mrs. Carbonese.

"Mrs. C., come with us!" Mike cried. "We're trying to save your life!"

The teacher turned to Mike with a frightened look. "You rude boy, I will *not* be your wife!"

Mike paused. "Oh, never mind, just run!"

Liz climbed onto the AV cart in the back of the room and kicked against the rear wall. *Whoosh!* In a second she was up by the door with Mike and Mrs. Carbonese. She jumped out into the hall and ran.

Clack-clack! Mrs. Carbonese struggled to keep up with the two kids.

A moment later the hallway was filled with potato-brained students, stumbling after them.

"We need to get you to safety, Mrs. C.,"

said Mike. Then he noticed a door down the hall, not far from the main school doors. "Yes! We'll hide you in Mr. Sweeney's supply closet!"

"But . . . but . . ." Mrs. Carbonese mumbled.

Before she could object, the two kids pushed her gently into the closet with the brooms and mops and cleaning fluids and shut the door.

"You'll be safer in there," Liz called through the door.

"But the smell!" came the muffled cry. "And it's dark in here!"

"Sorry!" cried Mike. "We'll be back for you — " But that was all he could get out. From behind him he heard something strange. Something horrible. Something musical.

Yo-he-ho! Yo-ho!
Yo-he-ho! Yo-ho!

When Mike turned around, he froze in terror.

Out of the shadows came Principal Bell,

Miss Lieberman, and Mr. Sweeney. They were pulling a long chain as they sang.

Yo-he-ho! Yo-ho!

Yo-he-ho! Yo-ho!

On the end of the long chain was one of the janitor's rolling buckets. And sitting in the bucket, an evil grin growing across his gnarly, bumpy skin, was —

"Potadio!" shrieked Mike. "They're treating him like some kind of king! He's already taken control of the school! What more does he want?"

The answer came with a sudden, terrifying, school-shattering noise.

BLAAAAAMMMMM!

The school's front doors blasted open and a cloud of thick brown dust blew into the main hall.

Out of the cloud rolled hundreds, thousands, hundreds of thousands of dirty brown potatoes!

"My new students!" cried Principal Bell.

"My floors!" cried Mr. Sweeney.

"My army!" cried King Spud.

The Horrible, Horrible Plan

Mike ducked behind the double doors of the cafeteria. Liz jumped down next to him.

"He called them his army!" Mike hissed.

The potatoes rolled across the floor and bowed before Potadio. "Come, my spudlets," the large potato said. "And listen to my wonderful, wonderful plan!"

Sparks shot off from the huge brain as the teachers pulled the giant vegetable's rolling bucket down the hall and off into the shadows.

"He's growing bigger every minute," said Liz.

Mike slumped to the floor. "Oh, man,

what have I done? I made this monster. And all I wanted was to be a scientist, an inventor."

Liz looked over at him. "Dr. Frankenstein was like that. Just a guy with a science project."

"Thanks for reminding me." Mike made a face. "Our lives, the school, our town, maybe the whole world, are at stake. And all because of me. Potadio is all brain. He's super smart. I have to stop him."

"*We* have to stop him, you mean," said Liz.

Mike managed a weak smile. "Thanks. I couldn't do it without you." But deep inside, he knew it was not going to be easy. He had messed things up big time. He had to make them right.

"First things first, Mike," said Liz. "We follow him. We need to find out what his wonderful, wonderful plan is."

Mike nodded. "Something tells me it's not going to be so wonderful." He looked at

Liz. "We have to make things normal. We have to."

She twisted her face a little. "Don't get carried away, Mike. This is Grover's Mill, remember? If we just get out of this alive, I'll be happy."

As the two friends crept down the hall into the darkness, Mike doubted whether they'd ever be happy again.

The dusty trail led to the school auditorium.

"Maybe he's putting on a show?" said Liz.

The two kids slipped through the rear doors of the auditorium and huddled in the back corner.

Hanging on the stage behind the podium was a giant poster. The potato brain's picture was on the poster, and written in giant letters above the picture were the words — King Spud.

"King?" whispered Mike. "I really don't like the sound of that. He used to be just a potato."

Behind the podium Sean, Jeff, and Holly were standing with the other students and teachers.

The potato army was murmuring and chattering in their seats. The lights went down and everyone began to applaud.

Mike tapped Liz on the shoulder and pointed to the front of the auditorium. The two kids crept quietly down a side aisle.

A moment later, a spotlight shined on the stage. The giant Potadio waddled up to the podium. He was even larger now, about four feet tall. He began to thump his long leafy sprouts on the podium.

"Humans!" he cried out. "All they want to do is eat us. For years we've lived in fear of the fork. Well, that's going to change — starting now!"

"Rmm! Rmm!" the potato army murmured.

Liz shook her head and sighed. "That's all we need in Grover's Mill. Giant vegetables with attitudes."

Thump! Thump! went the leafy sprouts. "No longer will we live under the ground like common vegetables!" King Spud shouted. "Follow me, my spudlets, and we'll conquer the world!"

Cheers echoed against the walls of the auditorium. Principal Bell stumbled over and set a large crown on the potato's head. Sparks flew up.

"Careful with the crown, Mr. Ding-dong Bell!" King Spud cried. "This brain is supercharged!"

"All hail King Spud!" announced the principal. Again the room rocked with applause.

"These lights! This crown!" King Spud announced loudly. "They make me wanna — sing!"

One of King Spud's leafy arms yanked the microphone from the podium and he waddled out to the middle of the stage. The spotlight followed him. He tipped his crown low on his forehead, curled his lips, and began.

I may not be so pretty,
  I'm sure not itty-bitty,
But I'm conquering your city
  'Cause I've got elec-tri-city!
  Oh, I'm the King —
  The King of everything!

Mike was stunned. "This is all my fault."

Liz nodded. "Well, it sure has gone way beyond potatoes and radios. King of *everything?*"

"This kind of stuff seems to happen a lot in Grover's Mill, doesn't it?" asked Mike.

Liz smiled. "The Zone, Mike. The center of galactic weirdness."

Yes, I'm the Big Bad King
  Of Everythiiiiiiiiing!

As Spud held that last long note, a horrible thing happened. The giant poster behind him disappeared, and there, in full color, was another large picture. A map.

"We're going on a trip!" shouted the royal

potato. His leafy sprouts unfurled and slapped the map again and again, pointing to a star on the east coast. "To the big city!"

Mike squinted. He knew that star.

"Next stop — Washington, DC!" King Spud proclaimed. "The capital of the Potato States of America!"

Liz Duffey, the Potato!

"*Rmmmmmm!*" The potato audience thundered. The spuds bounced in their seats.

"Let's beat it before the lights come up," said Mike. He and Liz slipped quietly out the back doors and out into the hall.

"Did you hear what he said?" cried Mike. "He's going to attack Washington! That's the capital of our country. The President! The Congress! The Supreme Court! Without them, we're doomed! We'd be totally out of control!"

"We haven't studied the Supreme Court yet," said Liz. "But I know what you mean."

The rumbling in the auditorium grew

louder.

"King Spud is sending out his brain waves again," said Mike. "His army's getting noisier."

Liz's eyes started to water. The tip of her nose twitched. Her chin quivered.

"But, hey, don't cry," said Mike. "I'm sure we'll figure something out."

"Cry?" Liz made a face at Mike. "I just need to blow my nose. This cold is killing me."

She took out a tissue and blew into it a couple of times. "Oh, this is great. Finally, my ears popped. It feels so good. And I can hear! I can actually hear — " Liz broke off. She stuck a finger in her ear and wiggled it. "What? Yes . . . yes . . . right away . . . *master!*"

Mike stepped back. "Whoa, Liz! What are you doing? You're not getting weird on me are you?"

Liz turned to him. Her eyes were glassy.

Mike stepped backward. "You're joking, right? Like, ha-ha, wouldn't it be funny if our brains were controlled by King Spud and — "

Liz stared at him but didn't focus on him.

"Yes, Michael Mazur. Ha. Ha," she droned. "I am very funny with joking. Weird is not what I am. I will not hurt you."

"Whoa," said Mike. "Who said anything about hurting?"

Liz didn't answer, but she stumbled down the hall to Mrs. Carbonese's room. A moment later, she was back and walking slowly toward Mike.

He moved away step by step. This is not good, he thought. If Liz's brain really was being controlled by King Spud, then he was all alone in this. And Mike was pretty sure he wouldn't be able to do it all alone. He needed Liz. A lot.

"Um, hey, Liz, remember the time when we fought that big dinosaur beast guy, Gorga? That was pretty fun, wasn't it?"

"Fun," Liz droned, nodding up and down.

She kept coming.

Rmmmmm! The rumbling from the auditorium was even louder now. The floor rocked.

Mike glanced both ways down the hall, looking for the best way to run. "And of course you remember how I sort of saved your life when Gorga lifted you off the ground?"

"Ground," repeated Liz. "I was born in the ground."

"Uh, no, actually, you weren't," said Mike. "You are not a vegetable. You're my friend, right? F-r-i-e-n-d. Remember?"

Liz still kept coming.

Mike kept backing away. "Okay, look," he said. "I'm not going to let this happen, Liz. It's too late for the rest of them, but not for us. We're the only ones left to stop King Spud. Well, there's Mrs. C., but I wouldn't expect that she could do much to stop King Spud, and — "

"Spud!" shouted Liz, jerking her right

hand up in the air in a fist. Then she opened her hand. In it was a small green box. Slowly, she pulled something white out of it.

Mike's eyes were fixed on what she was doing. This is all my fault, he thought. Totally.

Crack!

The box hit the floor. Liz brought the white thing up in front of her face. It was a dusty one-inch nib of chalk!

"So, Liz, you gonna do some math problems?" But Mike knew deep down that she didn't have math on her mind.

He shuddered.

Liz scratched her ears. "Yes, master!"

"Aw, you don't have to call me that," Mike said, still backing down the hall and glancing for the nearest door.

But he couldn't take his eyes off Liz for an instant. The gleam of a doorknob sparkled at the very corner of his eye. Yes! A door. A classroom. A window. Outside, home, TV, food.

The whole world of freedom spread out before him in a fraction of a second.

The door was about fifteen feet away. "Liz, remember the time — "

"Call me Spudlet ninety-nine." Then Liz took a deep breath and blew it out over the piece of chalk. A puff of white chalk dust floated toward Mike.

Rmmm! The auditorium thundered.

"Yes, master!" Liz said again. "Right now!"

Liz lowered the little white stick and held it out like a little white sword.

Then she charged at Mike.

A Cast of Thousands!

"**N**o!" Mike screamed. He ran for the doorknob. He jiggled it. It wouldn't turn. His hands kept slipping.

"Help!" he yelled. But there was no one left to help him.

Liz came closer and closer, pointing that chalk right at him like a weapon. Her eyes were weird. She was one of *them*! A potato-brain!

In that frightful instant, it hit Mike with the force of a Double Dunk donut hurled at great speed. Brain waves! He had to block the brain waves!

Mike finally gripped the knob and turned it.

It opened.

A wrinkled pink face popped out!

"Mrs. Carbonese!" Mike shrieked.

"The rude boy!" the teacher shrieked. She stuck her silver police whistle in her mouth and blew — hard!

Woooooooo!

Liz suddenly staggered back and slapped her ears hard. "What — ?"

Mike took a deep breath and blew on Liz's chalk.

Puff! A little cloud of white dust drifted back into Liz's face. She stopped. She squinted. She sneezed.

AAAA — CHOOOOO!

"Whoa — ugh!" snarled Liz, staring at the chalk in front of her nose. "My ears just plugged up big time! Hey, what's this chalk for?"

"Liz!" shouted Mike. "You're back! Boy, am I glad you're not a potato-brain anymore. Wait, you're not a potato-brain anymore, are you? I mean, uh, who's your king?"

Liz made a face. "Mike, we don't have kings here, we have presidents, and if we don't stop King Spud and his potato army, we won't even have one of those!"

Mike turned to Mrs. Carbonese and smiled. "Oh, yeah, she's back."

Suddenly — *BLAM!* The doors from the auditorium burst open and an army of potatoes poured into the hallway!

Mike gasped. The potatoes were bigger and noiser than before. They were growing features — just like King Spud.

Little mouths with sharp little teeth.

Little brains bulging on their heads.

"Let's get out of here before we're spud snacks!" Mike screamed.

Liz dashed for the doors at the end of the hall. "Come with us, Mrs. C.!"

"No, I don't miss the sea," the teacher said. "I quite like the desert, thank you, dear."

Mike almost laughed. Mrs. Carbonese was way hard-of-hearing, Liz's ears were blocked from her cold, and he had a problem with wax in his ears.

None of them could hear the brain waves.

That's why none of them were potato-brains!

"Hurry," he yelled, as he led the two humans out of the school to the rear parking lot.

Mike motioned across the lot. "Let's bolt for the fence and then through the woods and — "

ERRRRRRKK! A giant yellow school bus screeched around the flagpole and pulled to a sudden stop in front of the school.

At the wheel was — Rock Storm!

"Wait!" Mike whispered, sliding on the grass. He motioned for Liz and Mrs. Carbonese. "We have to find out what's with the bus."

The three crept quietly around the side of the school. They peered over a low stone wall next to the front lot.

The potato army crashed from the school

and tumbled out to the sidewalk. Then, all together, the dusty army turned their grinning, toothy faces to see King Spud emerge from the school.

Spud was nearly six feet tall now and almost as wide. He waddled very slowly. His big pink brain bulged high over his giant head. It sparked and sizzled with incredible brain power.

Principal Bell and Miss Lieberman helped him down the steps carefully, bowing all the way.

Rock Storm came over from the school bus. "Here to do your bidding, oh, giant master!"

"It's about time, fluffy boy!" snarled the enormous potato. Then he wrinkled his giant brain. "Wait, hold everything. I'm picking up some bad vibrations. Can it be? Oh, yeah! There are humans still among us!"

"*Rmmm! Rmmm!*" the crowd of spuds rumbled. They began looking around with their many eyes.

"I thought only corn had ears," Mike whispered from behind the wall. "It's like my Potadio grew some kind of supersonic computer chip in that huge brain of his."

"Hey!" cried King Spud, looking over the crowd. "Who said *chip*? Never — ever — say *chip* to a potato!"

Then the giant vegetable spotted the three heads peering over the wall and jabbed his leafy sprouts at them.

"Humans!" cried King Spud. "Get them!"

Mike gulped. "Uh-oh."

Humans — as in Cannonballs!

With an angry flick of his sprouts, King Spud sent Principal Bell, Miss Lieberman, Mr. Sweeney, Rock Storm, and all two hundred and ninety-eight W. Reid Elementary School students charging after Mike, Liz, and Mrs. Carbonese.

"I think it was something we said!" cried Mike. "Come on!" The three dashed over to the double doors of the school.

Rrrrrrr! The bus engine roared. Mike glanced back to see King Spud wedge himself into the driver's seat. "The ultimate field trip!" the potato leader cried. "To take over the world!"

Mike watched the school bus roar away.

"Get the humans!" shouted Principal Bell.

"Rmm-rmm!" cried Miss Lieberman.

In that instant, Mike realized he had to think of something quick. And when he raced into the gym, he knew what it was. "Only one thing can save us *and* stop King Spud!"

"It would be nice if you told us!" huffed Liz, helping Mrs. Carbonese try to run in her high-heeled shoes.

"That!" cried Mike, pointing to the giant catapult against the far wall.

"Whoa," said Liz, slowing down. "I think the wax must have gone to your brain. That thing almost killed me. There's no way we're using it!"

"Oh, yes we are!" Mike ran up to the catapult. He rolled it toward the back doors of the gym and into the lot behind the school.

Wham! The double gym doors flew open.

"Rmmm! Rmmm!" grumbled the angry mob of potato-brained humans as they made their way across the room.

"Hurry!" Mike grabbed Liz's hand and pulled her with him into the launcher bowl of the catapult.

"Rmmm!" The potato-brain teachers and students roared after them out into the parking lot. At the head of the mob were Sean, Holly, and Jeff, pointing and yelling, "Get them! They don't have numbers. They don't do the secret potato salute. They're not like us!"

"Mrs. C.!" cried Mike. "Hurry up and pull the lever!"

"Never mind the weather!" Mrs. Carbonese yelled. "You two kids better fly!"

She pulled the lever.

FWONG!

With incredible force, Mike and Liz were hurled like human cannonballs into the air.

"Whoa!" screeched Mike.

"Whoa!" screeched Liz.

The two kids shot up over the top of the gym, over the flagpole, over the school parking lot, and high over Main Street.

Mrs. Carbonese climbed up to the top of the catapult and kicked at the potato-brains with her high-heeled shoes.

"There's the bus," Mike cried out, whizzing fast over Grover's Mill. "We've got to stop it!"

"We've got to stop ourselves, too!" wailed Liz, as they just missed getting hooked by the giant fishing pole on the Baits Motel.

Then they started to drop. Fast.

WHAM! WHAM! Mike and Liz hit something. Something yellow and black. Something yellow and black and very hard. Mike opened his eyes.

"The school bus!" Mike shrieked. "We made it! We actually — "

Errrk! The bus swerved onto Main Street and picked up speed.

"Help!" cried Liz, nearly sliding off the top.

Mike quickly grabbed her by the wrist and yanked her back on. Then he started to crawl across the roof to the front. "Follow me. I saw this in a movie once."

"Not one of the school bus safety videos," Liz groaned as she made her way over to Mike. "But then, they probably weren't thinking Weird Zone when they made those videos!"

King Spud turned the wheel sharply and the bus veered up on the sidewalk.

"Whoooooa!" Mike nearly lost his grip this time. His legs went flying out and banged against the sign on Duffey's Diner.

"Watch out!" cried Liz, reaching out for him. "My mom paid a lot for that sign!"

In one incredible move, Mike swung back over the top of the bus and came down hard. With both feet he kicked on the middle of the front door.

Sssss! The door opened and Mike swung in. A second later, Liz jumped in next to him.

The first thing they heard was singing!

Five million spuds on the White House wall,
    Five million spuds on the wall!

If one of those spuds should happen to fall —

King Spud stopped singing. "What smells?"

Liz growled, "End of the road, sprout face!"

King Spud gave them an astonished look. "This bus is for potatoes only!" His bulging brain turned purple with rage. He twirled the giant steering wheel angrily.

The two kids lost their balance.

King Spud snarled, "Finish them off, boys!"

Snap! Snap! Thousands of little dusty jaws began to clack open and shut. A puff of brown dust filled the bus as the spudlet army leaped from their seats and tumbled forward.

"Stampede!" screamed Liz.

"Potato stampede!" screamed Mike.

The Last (Vegetable) Stand!

"*Rmmmmm! Rmmmmm!*" The potatoes charged forward, their teeth snapping and clacking.

At that moment, something caught Mike's eye. Rolling out from under the driver's seat was a little crumpled ball of paper.

Mike reached for it. "Yes!" he grinned. It was a greasy, dirty, stained Jolly Meal french fry bag! Just like the one he'd slipped on that morning.

Mike held it up to show Liz.

Liz made a face. "I know you're hungry, but — "

"Watch this!" Mike thrust the bag right

into the faces of the attacking spuds. "French fries!"

"Eeeee!" the dusty potatoes stopped rolling and jerked away in fear.

"Think you're clever, human boy?" snarled the king of the spuds. He jammed one of his leafy legs down on the gas pedal.

ROAR! The bus shot straight down Main Street toward the desert.

Mike slammed against the front seat. "Liz, he's going for the open road! For the highway! For Washington, DC, the capital of our country! The President! The Congress! The Supreme — "

"I know, I know, I know!" shrieked Liz, kicking some smaller potatoes to the back of the bus.

"Here!" Mike gave her the french fry bag. She waved it at the spudlets as Mike jumped up and grabbed the large wheel.

"Get off me, two eyes!" cried King Spud. The vegetable's giant brain heaved and twitched.

"Got . . . to . . . stop . . . you!" Mike gasped

as he spun the wheel hard and swatted the leafy sprouts. The blubbery potato nearly swallowed him up.

Errrrrck! The bus wound around in a tight circle, crashed through the gate of the Plan Nine Drive-in and bounced into the parking lot.

The sign over the ticket booth read, *Attack of the Very Big Kitchen Utensils!*

Mr. Vickers the movie director came running out of the ticket booth. He carried a giant movie prop in the shape of a fork.

"Oh, trying to check if I'm *done*?" screeched King Spud. "Well, I'm not *done* yet!" He pushed Mike away and spun the wheel sharply.

"Now, there's a big potato!" Mr. Vickers cried, leaping out of the way. "Hey, wait. Can you act?"

"Sure, I can act," King Spud screamed out. "I can act crazy!" He pushed Mike away and sped out of the parking lot and back up Main Street.

The bus took a sharp left back onto School Road.

CRASH! It leaped the sidewalk and mangled the W. Reid Elementary School flagpole into a pretzel. The bus stopped dead.

"Destroy that school once and for all!" shouted King Spud to his angry army.

Mike and Liz leaped from the bus and ran, a horde of toothy spudlets hot on their heels.

Inside the school, the two kids tore down the hall and turned the corner. They slid to a stop.

Out of the shadows in front of them stepped Jeff, Sean, and Holly. Their eyes were all glassy. They blocked the way and stumbled forward.

"Okay, Liz," mumbled Mike, backing away. "I know this is sort of my fault. But I'd be happy for some suggestions right about now. Got any?"

Liz glanced around. Behind them was the door to the nurse's office. Suddenly she snapped her fingers. "Actually, I do!" She pulled Mike into the nurse's office and began searching around.

The three potato-brained kids blocked the door and started to close in. "Knock-knock," droned Sean. "Any humans here to attack?"

Liz whirled around, smiling. She held up a handful of fluffy white cotton balls in her hands.

"Okay," murmured Mike, "but you'll have to throw those really hard to stop these guys."

Liz pushed Mike behind her and in a flash she pulled the cotton balls apart and stuffed little bits into the six ears of her three potato-brained friends.

The three potato-brains stopped their attack.

"Hey, I can't hear," said Sean. "But I feel pretty good about it."

"Me, too," said Holly. "Cool!"

"What happened to that weird sound?" Jeff asked. "I was sort of getting used to it."

"Long story," said Mike, dashing out into

the hall and starting for the main office. "Now, come on!" he shouted so they could hear. "I have a plan, but we have to hurry!"

Mike knew what he had to do. He took a right off the main hall and raced into the main office.

Mr. Bell was sitting alone in the inner office, scribbling pictures of potatoes with crowns on them. "Yes, wonderful master! Of course, oh, large-brained leader!"

Mike stepped quietly over to the PA system in the outer office. The announcement microphone stood on the counter next to the control box.

Next to it was a tape player.

"We've got to break those bad sound waves that everybody is hearing," Mike whispered to his friends. "It's the only way to free them from Spud's mind control!"

"Hurry," said Liz. "They're getting closer."

Mike read the name of the tape in the player. *"Classic Food Songs of the Great Crooners?"* He made a face. "Is this all

there is?"

"Play it, Mike," Liz urged. "Play it loud!"

Mike moved the PA microphone over to the tape player and hit the play button. Instantly, trombones and saxophones roared into the PA.

And a singer began to sing.

When the moon hits your toe
Like a big po-ta-to — it's so sore, eh?

Mr. Bell jumped from his desk. "Miss Lieberman, may I have the next dance — Hey, owww!"

The principal slapped his hands over his ears and gave a pained look. Suddenly, he frowned. "That high-pitched sound!" he said. "It's gone!"

"Come, sir," said Mike, respectfully. "We've got a school to defend!"

"Quite right!" the principal agreed. "Let's go!"

But when they jumped out into the hall, the hall was filled with mad potatoes.

Hopping mad potatoes!

"Ahem!" boomed Mr. Bell. "They're here."

King Spud waddled up through the crowd. His bulging brain nearly skimmed the ceiling.

The PA blared out.

French fries, shining on me!
  Nothing but french fries, do I see!

Spud's big brain rippled and twitched in rage. "Turn that hideous music down now!" he cried, thrusting his leafy sprouts at the humans. His brain nearly popped. It bulged, it throbbed.

"I don't think so," said Mike, standing firm.

"We don't think so, either," said Liz, standing with Jeff, Sean, and Holly.

"Quite right," said Principal Bell. "I, as well."

"So, my supersonic brain-control waves don't work, eh?" King Spud said. "Okay, then, no more Mr. Nice Potato! We'll just eat you! How's that for a switch? Potatoes eat people!"

The big brain turned purple with anger.

Mike's own brain started to twitch and get mad. "I've only been in this school for a little while. I know it's way weird, but I'm not going to let it be taken over by a blubbery vegetable!"

Mike stepped forward. "King Spud, your brain wave days are over!"

"Never!" the potato leader cried out. "Bite them, spudlets! Bite them all up!"

Weird (Zone) Science

"**G**ET THEM NOW!" King Spud screamed, and his little potatoes leaped at the humans, their sharp teeth chomping as they hurled themselves at sneakers and ankles.

"Food fight!" yelled Mike, tearing a spudlet from his pants leg and hurling it screaming across the hall.

Suddenly — *Wham!* The science door banged open and Rock Storm charged over with a microphone. "How about you kids fight, and I do a play-by-play for our radio audience?"

Liz shot a look at Mike. "That's help?" Then she swung around and drop-kicked a handful of potatoes from the water fountain.

"And they're off!" said Rock Storm. "A squad of spunky students is battling down the main hall, while a horde of hungry vegetables attacks them at every turn!"

But the W. Reid Elementary School kids and teachers fought back while the PA played on!

I've got cheese — under my skin!

Mike and Liz dashed for the corner of B-wing to head off a bunch of angry spuds who charged out of the art room with war paint on.

Suddenly — *Whack! Splat! Whack! Splat!*

Brown lumps smashed on the far wall and slumped to the floor. The little spuds lay still.

"Hey," said Mike. "Looks like we've got some major backup." They turned the corner.

Mrs. Carbonese was tossing up spuds

and whacking them against the wall with a broom. "I just don't like the look of them," she said.

Whack! Splat!

"I have to say it," cried Liz. "What a school!"

Mike nodded proudly. "The W. Reid spirit!"

But King Spud called his troops together and they drove the humans into the gym. Science project tables crashed to pieces as the vegetable army attacked.

"The final battle!" cried King Spud, his brain reaching almost as high as the basketball hoops.

Liz pulled Mike back through the tables. "We'd better think of something, and quick! Potadio just keeps getting bigger and bigger!"

As King Spud laughed a horrible laugh, his giant brain buzzed and shot sparks into the air.

"That's it!" Mike cried. "Electricity! King Spud is an amazing, giant, powerful battery. He's full of electric power. Probably thousands of volts!"

"Yeah, so?" said Liz, kicking some spuds away from her ankles. They scurried off.

"I read all about electricity for my project," said Mike. "I nearly shorted out the whole neighborhood. Maybe we can short out King Spud! Now if only we had — "

Then Mike spotted something. "Jeff's Gizmo!" He and Liz fought their way over to the strange machine. "Remember when Jeff ran this? The whole school went black. It's perfect!" In a matter of seconds, Mike had formed a plan. He explained it to Liz.

"That sounds like one of my weird plans," said Liz. Then she smiled. "I like it. It just might work."

Mike grabbed the Gizmo's electrical cord. He looked up. "Hey, King Dud!"

The fat potato leader turned angrily. He squeezed between the tables toward Mike. "We could have been a great team, kid. But no, you didn't want to be a potato. So now I have to destroy you. Start thinking of your last words, skinny!"

Mike stood his ground, hiding the cord behind him. The blubbery potato waddled closer.

Then, from across the room, came Liz's call. "Hey, Brainiac!" She roared toward King Spud on her Motorboard. "Here I come!"

The giant potato turned. A look of horror crossed his wrinkled face as he saw Liz tearing between the tables right for him.

"No!" King Spud cried out. He tried to get out of the way, but he was so blubbery he couldn't move fast enough. His brain sparked in anger!

POOOMF! Liz slammed against the giant vegetable. He wobbled. He teetered. He tottered.

At that instant, Mike dived forward and thrust the Gizmo cord right into the king-size potato!

ZZZZ! KRRR! NNNN! Jeff's do-nothing Gizmo finally did something!

Sparks exploded everywhere! Giant zig-zag bolts of electricity blasted from King Spud across the gym to all the little spuds — they all hopped and sizzled!

"I'm frying!" shrieked the potato king.

KA — BLAMMMMMM!

The ceiling lights crackled and popped! The school went dark. The music stopped.

Everything was quiet.

THWUMP! The giant potato hit the ground.

"And the big brain goes down!" Sean whooped.

"Oh!" gasped Holly. "The smell!"

"Like a Jumbo Jolly Meal with Extra Double-*Fried* Fries!" Jeff called out.

The battle was over. A towering pile of toasted spuds lay all around their fallen leader. Mike, Liz, Holly, Sean, and Jeff stepped over to the giant shape.

King Spud groaned. He tried to speak. As Mike leaned over to hear, he remembered how he had done the same thing earlier that day.

"Oh, the horror of it all!" King Spud sputtered. "But hear me now. I vow, the potato kingdom will rise again!"

The dusty brown lips quivered and fell silent.

All his eyes closed at once.

Rock Storm stuck his microphone in Mike's face. "Well, son," he boomed. "In a word, what do you think made the big potato brain go bad?"

Mike thought about that for a while. "I only know one thing. Even potatoes are too complicated to be understood by just a couple of words."

"Birds?" said Mrs. Carbonese.

"Ahem!" boomed Principal Bell.

"My floor!" shrieked Mr. Sweeney.

"How's my hair?" asked Rock Storm.

For a long time the five friends just nodded at the big wide truth of it all.

"Oh, no!" shrieked Liz, pointing to the door.

Everyone whirled around to see Miss

Lieberman taping a sheet of paper to the wall.

Liz read it. "Next week's menu. Potato soup. Potato pie. Potato salad. Potato skins. Potato chips. Potato burgers. Po-tato cubes. Potatoes with cheese. Potatoes without cheese. Potato butter and jelly sandwiches."

"King Spud was right," said Holly. "Potatoes will rise again. And again and again and again."

Sean turned to Liz. "By the way, thanks for the cotton ball thing." He yanked the fluffy white puffs from his ears just as —

Brrrrring! — the dismissal bell rang.

"Ah, my favorite sound," said Sean. "School's over!"

Bong! went the giant donut clock on the top of the Double Dunk Donut Den.

Sssss! went the giant pan on the top of Usher's House of Pancakes.

"And those are my favorite sounds," said Mike, striding out through the school doors to the sidewalk in front. "Anybody hungry?"

Liz made a face at him. She looked at her friends. "Well . . . after all that, I don't know."

"Oh, come on," said Mike with a grin. "How about something different. Something unusual. After all, we do live in the Weird Zone!"

THE WEIRD ZONE

#6 ™

BIZARRE
EERIE
HILARIOUS

Written and Directed by Tony Abbott

What has a huge gray dome,
eight slimy tentacles, and a bad attitude?
It's Gigantopus from Planet X—on the attack
in Grover's Mill! Can Holly and her fearless
friends come up with a totally amazing plan
to stop the creepy creature?

Gigantopus from Planet X!

THE WEIRD ZONE #6
by Tony Abbott

WZT696